MW01108203

# Dear Bob

*The Misadventures of Petunia Pottersfeild.*

Copyright ©2016 by TP Keane

www.tpkeane.com

Massachusetts, USA

First Edition

Printed in the United States of America

Cover Design by TP Keane

ISBN 13: 978-0-9971793-2-3
ISBN 10: 0-9971793-2-5

To my wonderful niece, Natasha, whose boundless imagination and beautiful laughter has inspired my world of fairies.

## Chapter 1 – Summer's end

Dear Bob,

Yes, that's right. I've named you Bob. It's my eleventh birthday today and my mother has surprised me with you. I guess she knew I wasn't having much luck making friends with the other children in my class and thought it would be a good idea to write in a diary.

"It's almost like having a best friend you can talk to and share your feelings with," she said. I don't know if she's right, but if you are meant to be a friend of sorts then I can't very well call you *Diary* now, can I? It would be like calling my pet ladybug *Insect* instead of *Daisybell*.

Well, I guess if we are to be friends then I should introduce myself properly. My name is Petunia Pottersfield and, as I've mentioned, I am eleven-years-old. I live in a little village called Furrow Grove and I suppose it's as unremarkable as any other fairy ring. The mushroom houses circling the town are cosy and warm, and for the most part look exactly the same as one another. Some are lopsided, some are stretched tall, while others look as though a fat toad squashed them. But all have red tops and crooked stick chimneys that waft delicious smells of cooking all day long.

I live in the house furthest away from my school and for that I'm glad. I don't like school very much, or rather it doesn't like me. I guess you could say that we'd both be happy never to see each other again.

For some reason, that I've never been bothered to find out, the townsfolk in Furrow Grove also have a uniform of sorts; we all wear red. I don't know why that is exactly, but that is the way it has always been and, I expect, always will be. Nothing much changes around here.

"So how am I supposed to know which fairy you are?" I hear you ask. I suppose my one distinguishing feature is the mass of curly hair on top of my head. It kind of juts out in all directions and my parents are forever asking me if I remembered to brush it that morning, despite the fact that I usually still had my brush in my hand. I am forever swallowing the dishevelled mop on windy days too; it just flies right into my mouth. My mother tries her best to tie it out of the way, but it's just so unruly. She and I have the same hair, but even her skilled twists and turns with bobby pins are no match for it. It just won't be tamed.

If you look carefully underneath my nest of hair then you will see my dark green eyes peering out. My father has the same eyes, something of a rarity in our village apparently. Everyone else I know has brown, blue, lilac, or amber. But the oddity of my eyes is just one *more* thing that makes me stand out, and I hate them. I don't want to stand out. I just want to be like the rest of the kids in my class. I just want to be normal.

Alas, it seems that I am anything but. In case you haven't gathered I am not very popular. I suppose it's not due to the fact that my eyes are an unusual colour, or because I have something grotesque growing out of me either like a great, big wart on my head (Lucas Moonbeam in my class had that once, head warts can be nasty and very stubborn). And while my wings are the same shape and size as the rest of my classmates, for some reason mine are broken.

In whatever way I was made, the outside of me looks like an average fairy but inside, everything feels backwards. Have you ever felt, Bob, that no matter what you do or how hard you try to do things, they always come out wrong? Have you ever memorised spells until you knew them backward, but when you recite them the opposite thing happens? Like for instance, I tried to attract a butterfly in the school yard the other day, and I know I said the right words. But, wouldn't you know it, a great big, slimy earthworm appeared instead. It seems that no matter what I do, or how hard I work at not being me, it always turns out disastrously.

I remember my first flight—my mother and her frilly knickers remember it very well too. I guess I must have been about four-years-old when I first tried out my wings (yes, I know. I was a late bloomer, no laughing please). I was out in the garden playing with Daisybell and I suppose the wind might have been a little strong when I unfurled my wings to catch the breeze. My mother was hanging out the laundry behind me when I took off into the air like an autumn leaf in a tornado. I tumbled head first into her best pair of frilly knickers and ripped them nearly in half.

I will never forget the embarrassment of hanging upside-down on the washing line with my head poking out of one of the leg holes. My mother just laughed and told me that it was lucky I landed there instead of on the hard rocks below. But I'm not quite sure that it *was* that lucky. I think I would have rather landed on the rocks because for the next three years my older brother, Blackhawk, kept calling me "knicker-brains".

I can't say for sure when my older brother started calling me names, but I can't remember a time when he didn't. My mother said it's because he was jealous when I was born. Up until then, he had been the only child and my mother and father lavished him with affection and praise. I'm sure it might have been the initial reason he called me names, but after a while it seemed like he didn't need a reason.

He had become embarrassed of me. I suppose I don't blame him really. After all, he *is* the "golden boy" of the neighbourhood. He is the tallest and strongest in his class, his magic skills rival that of any of the teachers, and he is hands down the fastest flyer in the village. It's no wonder he doesn't want people to know we are related.

I can say, without a shadow of a doubt, that my brother and I are polar opposites of each other in every sense of the phrase. I am thinner, weaker, and shorter than most of my classmates. My magical abilities are nothing short of a danger to the world, and I look like a drunken bumble bee when I fly. I can't help it really. My father says that I'm still growing into myself and it will just take time. But it's been eleven years now and I'm still waiting for it to happen.

Even this morning, on my birthday, I tried to use my magic to open my curtains, but only managed to set them on fire. As I watched my parents running around dowsing the flames with water, I knew that this year was probably going to be the same as all the rest. I knew it because every year on my birthday, Bob, I try to open the curtains using magic… just to see if I have grown into them yet. And every year it ends with the same result.

My parents have gotten so used to it now that on the night before my birthday they leave a small bucket of water outside my door. "Just in case," they say. But I know what their thinking, I am a walking catastrophe and I always will be. I love my parents. They're so kind and loving, and I know they love me too. But sometimes I get the feeling that they wish I could be more like Blackhawk. I don't blame them.

This is probably why I don't have many friends either, Bob. Not many people want to hang out with someone who might accidently blow them up when she sneezes. But I did have a friend once, her name was Luna Farrow.

It was just before I started school and my mother thought it would be a good idea to make a friend before I went. So, like most parents would, she set up a playdate with one of the other children. I suppose it might have been a good idea for any *normal* fairy, but I'm afraid it didn't turn out so well for Luna.

They left us happily playing together in the garden, but when they came back to check on us... that's when the shrieking started. At some point in our playdate Luna and I had had a row and I accidently turned her into a green, warty toad. Blackhawk tells me that even to this day Luna still walks with a hop in her step. I honestly didn't mean it, and even to this day I'm not quite sure how I did it. But that was the last playdate I ever had, and she was my last friend too.

I'm not angry with the other kids for not wanting to hang out. I mean, who would want to be friends with someone like me? I truly am a disaster waiting to happen.

Even my potions teacher, Mrs. Scarrowtree, is wary of teaching me. She's a rather severe looking fairy with a pinched, red face and small brown eyes that make you think you're staring into a fire with two dark coals at its centre. She doesn't half make me nervous, you know. She also makes all of the other children wear acorn helmets and padded suits when I'm in the class. Even more humiliating is my flight teacher who does the opposite; he makes *me* wear the protective gear in case I should accidently fly into a thistle.

But it isn't fair, Bob! I don't know why I can't be like all the other children in my class. I don't know why my brain puts the wrong ingredients into the cauldron during potions, or why my wings won't fly me in a straight line. All I've wanted for as long as I can remember is just to be normal and to not stick out like a weed amongst the roses.

I guess that I am lucky in a way though. No matter how bad things get, at least I have Daisybell to talk to… and now you too. I suppose my mother was right. It's good to talk to someone, even if that someone isn't real and never answers back. So, I'll keep writing and

hope that I will soon grow into my magic.
Maybe this year *won't* be so bad after all.

Sincerely,
Petunia Pottersfield.

## Chapter 2 – Autumn onset

Dear Bob,

Well, I've managed it again! It's been about two weeks since I wrote to you last and so much has happened since then that it's hard to know where to begin. I suppose it's best to start where I left off.

After a depressingly dull birthday party, where the only guests were Daisybell and my family, I decided that I would study extra hard for my upcoming potions exam. I suppose I was so sick of being an outcast that I wanted to make sure I could at least create a potion that wouldn't accidently give anyone donkey teeth, or rabbit ears.

"That's a very sensible and mature thing to do; study hard for your exam," I hear you say. But it wasn't. It was the biggest mistake I have ever made and one I never intend on repeating again.

The horror of what unfolded was beyond anything that our history books have ever recorded, and it was all *my* fault. If I wasn't a pariah before this incident, then I certainly am now. Oh, I can't tell you how awful I feel, Bob: Humiliated, embarrassed and most of all ashamed.

I studied and recited all of the ingredients for the potion over and over in my head for a week until I was saying them in my sleep. I was fully sure that there was *no* way I could mess this one up. I even practice measuring out the proper quantities to make sure that I could do that too. Of course, as a student, I'm not allowed to make the actual potion outside of the classroom ... for obvious reasons ... so instead I used water and dried herbs as a substitute.

On the morning of my exam, I walked past the cute mushroom houses of our fairy ring and tried my hardest to give off an air of confidence. I waved hello to my neighbours, who cautiously waved back, and slid happily along a slimy trail left by a slug. All the way to school, I slid, (collecting some fresh slim in a jar as I went) confident that everything was going to turn out great. But as I stood outside of the large mushroom schoolhouse, the reminders of my past failures sprung to mind and let doubt creep back in.

I started to imagine how it would all go wrong, Bob. I started to tell myself that what I was about to do was *not* a good idea. I should have listened to myself.

Despite my nerves, the morning went quiet well. I spent my first period with Mr. Tumbleseed, who teaches the Global Knowledge class. I love his class because I don't have to do anything other than sit there and listen. Even *I* couldn't mess-up in that class.

Mr. Tumbleseed teaches us about things outside of the village walls and the dangers of getting caught by eagles, dogs, or even worse… a Bigfoot. I had never seen a Bigfoot before, but from what I heard they are the most dangerous creatures ever created and one should always steer clear of their gigantic feet or risk getting squashed. According to Mr. Tumbleseed, we fairies are so insignificantly small to these Bigfoot that the threat of death by squashing is a very real one.

It's hard to imagine their colossal size when all you ever see is a wall of tall grass blades surrounding the village. Only adult fairies are allowed to leave the fairy ring. But I overheard whispered stories from some of the Elders in our ring, about fairies getting caught and even eaten by these beasts. You'd think that the stories would make me scared, but they don't. In fact, they only made me more curious.

However horrific and deadly these outside creatures seemed to be, I had developed an unhealthy obsession with them. I daydreamed constantly about meeting one and vanquishing them to prove I'm not such a ding-bat. I suppose only someone like me, who is drawn to disaster, would.

I've often thought about peaking over the tall grass blades to have a look, but apparently it wouldn't have done me any good. Bigfoots are said to dwell in large stone castles far, far away from our little village of Furrow Grove. The only thing I have ever seen from the outside world was the occasional field mouse trundling through the village by accident. Of course, anything larger than an ant would set the town's alarms ringing and we would all be hustled indoors by the F.P.A.—the Fairy Protection Agency.

Within a matter of seconds the F.P.A. would clear any evidence of our existence. They would then hide in strategic locations around the village, ready to pounce on the oblivious traveller should they decide to chew through a mushroom and into someone's living room.

The F.P.A. are the heroes of the village and I do admire their work. They are all strong, brave, and the fastest flyers I have ever seen. I think Blackhawk want's to join them when he graduates fairy school. Knowing him, he will probably end up their captain within a few short months. I know I could never be part of the F.P.A. no matter how hard I tried. I am too much of a screw-up.

But I was determined that I would change how people saw me through hard work alone, even if it only made me less of a danger. And that's probably what led me to make the biggest mistake of my life.

You see, Bob, the potion I was reciting wasn't the one that was on the exam. Stupid me, I decided that if I could create a more powerful potion, one that we hadn't been shown yet, it would prove that I wasn't such an unbelievable jinx. While the other children were turning a dandelion into a rose, I had another idea… an insane idea now that I look back.

I wasn't going to transmorph any silly old flower. *Oh no*! I had to go and decide to create a living creature from the fresh snail slime I had collected that morning. I was meant to create a miniature bird that we could care for in our classroom. I thought it would be a nice gesture, seeing as how I was responsible for the last one escaping.

I honestly don't know what I was thinking.

Whilst Mrs. Scarrowtree was busy examining the other heavily-padded students work, I whipped up my potion in a matter of seconds. I don't know what went wrong. Perhaps it was the fact that I couldn't see what I was doing through my shock of curly hair, or maybe my hands went faster than my brain and I put the ingredients in in the wrong order. But whatever I did, I messed up… again.

My cauldron began to wobble as the black liquid inside bubbled uncontrollably. I tried to hide it by throwing a large cloth over it, but the liquid just kept growing and growing. Soon it oozed out from under the cloth and spilled over the table. I tried to call Mrs. Scarrowtree before it all went hideously wrong, but I guess she didn't hear me.

It wasn't long before my creation raised its towering, gelatinous body and slid onto the floor with a thunderous *plop*. That's when the horror truly began!

It seemed, or so Mrs. Scarrowtree told me afterward, that had I mixed some dried carnivorous plant extract in with my ingredients by mistake. It gave my monster a taste for meat, as well as anything else that crossed its path.

Oh, it was horrible, Bob. It slid around the classroom with its dripping arms outstretched, trying to grab the other children. It managed to catch Lilly Sudan, lifting her clean off her feet and into its gaping mouth. Thankfully she was wearing her acorn helmet because that's all that my monster managed to swallow before the F.P.A. showed up and pulled her out with a sickening *sloop* noise.

Oh Bob, I wanted to crawl into the ground and pretend like it had never happened. Everyone was crying and staring at me once the monster left. When their parents came to collect their trembling children, they were so angry that I thought they might actually try to curse me. They all looked so cross, everyone that is except for my parents.

Although they didn't say anything to me exactly, I could see it in my parent's eyes. They were embarrassed and ashamed. They whisked me out of school almost as soon as they arrived, apologising in whispered voices to everyone as we passed. I haven't been back to school since.

It took the F.P.A. two days to track down my slippery beast and it created all manner of destruction before they did. It slimed the neighbourhood streets until it looked like the frost fairy had melted all over the place. It ate all of my neighbours, Mr. Buddlesworth, best vegetables, and worst of all it slid through the underground mushroom tunnels and ate all of our winter supplies. Oh Bob, I don't know what I'm going to do. I can't go back to school, everyone will hate me. But I can't hide at home forever either... or can I?

Miserably,
Petunia Pottersfield.

## Chapter 3 – Mid-autumn

Dear Bob,

Oh Bob! I'm so excited I just can't tell you. I know this is a big change from my last time writing to you, but I have just been on the most wonderful adventure of my life. I don't have the words to tell you how exhilarating and spectacular it was, but I'll try my best.

After my last debacle in the potions exam, and the havoc that followed, I spent about three weeks locked inside my bedroom. I honestly was so ashamed and humiliated that I had fully intended on living out the rest of my life there. I didn't want to ever show my face in Furrow Grove again and I had utterly sworn off using magic of *any* kind.

Of course, Blackhawk thought it was a great idea and called me names like "the jinx of Furrow Grove" and "blunder butt". He thought he was hilarious and laughed long and hard every time he thought of it.

My parents, however, had other ideas on what I should do. They both decided that I needed to get out of the house and start showing my face around town again.

"A fairy can get very used to the dark and turn all kinds of peculiar, like old man Duckweed down the road," they said.

Old man Duckweed is a nasty old fairy. He doesn't dress in red like everyone else; he dresses in tattered, smelly black robes that matches his black eyes. His long, matted beard, dangling in front of him, only serves to accentuate his hunched back as he hobbles through Furrow Grove with a twisted walking stick. He also seems to have an intense hatred for all things happy and… well… living really.

Most fairies wouldn't mind if some kids happened to walk too close to their flower patch. But old man Duckweed seems to go out of his way to shoo the children away, even if they're nowhere near his garden. He throws rocks at fairies flying past and shouts at anyone who dares brush too close to his house.

People say that he was once the happiest fairy in all of Furrow Grove, and his home was something the whole neighbourhood would have aspired to. But not anymore.

His garden was thick with weeds and his mushroom seemed miserable to have him living in it. Where the roof should be red with large white dots, it is as dark and shrivelled looking as old man Duckweed. Where it all went wrong, I don't know. Nobody does really, but somewhere along the way he turned into a bitter and twisted fairy with a hatred for all things happy.

I don't want to turn into an old woman Duckweed, Bob. I definitely don't. All I want to do is to keep everyone safe from *me,* and that's it. Regardless of my resolve, however, my parent's persistence and warnings of lunacy convinced me otherwise, and I'm very glad they did. Oh Bob, I can't tell you how glad I am!

Yesterday morning I agreed to venture out with my father. He works in the underground root tunnels (yes the ones my monster destroyed) and he wanted me to see what he did for the fairy community. It's a very important job, one that I am sure I would mess up if I were in charge of it.

Beneath our fairy ring is a tunnel of mushroom roots. It creates a mound just under the soil in the shape of a circle. When winter comes and the mushroom houses die, we fairies move below the ground and into these warmer tunnels. I remember quite a few winters spent underground, but I never really thought about why we did it until yesterday?

Anyway, my father is in charge of stocking the tunnels with enough food for all of the families for the winter. We don't go above ground into the cold because our wings have a tendency to freeze. Well, everyone that is except for the frost fairy, whose job it is to bring the cold.

After a half a year of neglect, the fleshy, rounded walls can get damaged with other roots growing in and insects burrowing through them. My father has the added responsibility of reinforcing the tunnel walls too. Without him, and the other tunnel workers, we would be lost to the harsh, cold winds of winter.

I can't tell you how much guiltier it made me feel about my monster and the damaged he had done. I understood now why people were *so* cross with me. I could have doomed us all. Thankfully there was still enough time left in the autumn to restock, but it will mean a lot of overtime for my poor father and his co-workers.

As interesting as his job sounds, and as horrible as it might be to say, that isn't why I am so excited. You see, Bob, I also went with my mother to *her* job and I finally got my wish to venture outside of the fairy ring. My mother, you see, is a magic collector. She and a few others are responsible for collecting enough magic dust for the entire fairy ring. And as you know, we use magic for everything.

"Where does she get the magic?" I hear you ask. I didn't know either until yesterday.

Magic comes from dreams. Yes, that's right from dreams, Bob. You see everything dreams, fairies, birds, dogs, horses, and even Bigfoots. But apparently the best way to get a lot of magic dust is from Bigfoots. My mother says it's because they don't use the magic they have inside of them at all. It means they have a surplus supply of it that we can syphon when they dream.

My mother's job is to collect this dust. Of course there are different types of magic dust too, good dreams produce good magic and bad dreams make bad magic. I never knew that before. I just assumed that magic was magic, and whether or not it was good or bad depended on the user. Kind of like how that nasty old sprite, Duckweed, likes to send a spark of electricity toward some of the *larger* fairies, and yell them to get some exercise. He's nothing short of bad no matter what kind of dust he has if you ask me.

According to my mother, a fairy is never to use dust from bad dreams because it can change them. She didn't go into any details with me, but from her expression I gathered that it would be a really, really, really, *really* bad idea.

Last night, at the stroke of midnight, my mother and the other magic collectors lifted a large container from the centre of Furrow Grove village. It was made out of four broad leaves, woven together and looped around some carrying poles. It didn't look heavy but once it was filled to the brim with magic dust, it was a struggle for them to lift it.

My mother, of course, wasn't oblivious to my lack of flying skills and she tethered me to her with a long rope. It was a little embarrassing, but I was too excited to care. It helped that I had the cover of darkness and, thankfully, the other magic collectors didn't seem to notice… or at least they pretended not to.

I have never felt as alive as I did at that moment when we took off over the tall grass. I felt free and a little naughty, like I was doing something which I shouldn't be doing. But I didn't really care.

After some time, and with my acorn helmet securely fastened, my mother undid the rope to give me some freedom. Oh, how I loved it, Bob. I had all of this space to fly and stretch my wings and I only bumped into things occasionally. I think I was flying even faster than my mother could and she found it difficult to keep up. On more than one occasion, she had to shout at me to slow down. But I couldn't help forgetting.

The breeze through my curly hair, the crisp coldness over my arms and legs, the silvery light of the moon cast over a huge expanse of land. Oh Bob, it was such a wonderful feeling.

We flew over streams and beneath the colossal arms of giant oak trees, which I bumped into occasionally. We skimmed over the tops of enormous animals covered in a soft white fluff. One tried to eat me. We ducked and dived between corn stalks and at one point, I nearly got trodden on by something called a cow. Oh, but I didn't mind. It was wonderful, Bob! I could finally see all of the stars stretch toward the edge of the world and they, were, beautiful.

Not only did I see the stars but I also saw something else too. Something which I'm not sure will give me nightmares, but rather fantastical dreams. I saw a Bigfoot. Well, actually I saw a lot of Bigfoots.

We flew up to one of their enormous houses under the cover of the tree's shadows. Oh my goodness, Bob, it was *huge*. You could have stacked a hundred fairies on top of one another and they still wouldn't have reached the roof. The walls were made out of some kind of rock and enormous windows stretched higher than the length of our whole village.

I stayed by the window whilst my mother worked; perched, untethered, outside with my nose pressed up against the window pane. In every room that they flew into, there was always a humongous Bigfoot snoring so loudly that I could feel the vibrations through the glass. At one point, one of the other magic collectors nearly got sucked into the behemoths mouth when it snored.

I'm not sure if I could do my mother's job because you have to be very, very quiet, you see—so as not to wake the Bigfoot. And I have a bothersome habit of knocking things over. My mother told me that if a Bigfoot were to catch you, they would trap you, dissect you, or make you do magic for them for the rest of your life.

I didn't like the sound of that, not one bit. But when I looked at the Bigfoots, I didn't think that they were all that different from us. Although they didn't have wings and they were about a bazillion times bigger than us, they still had two arms, two legs, a head, and everything else that we have.

But it got me wondering. Perhaps, if it wasn't for the secrecy, maybe one day the fairies and the Bigfoots *could* be friends. It's a silly idea, Bob. Another one of my hair brained ideas that will only get me into trouble, I'm sure. I suppose that we fairies have kept ourselves secret for thousands of years for a very good reason.

But Bob, what happened next was spectacular, wondrous, and mystifying all at once. My mother and the other magic collectors hovered over the Bigfoots head and recited a magical spell. I couldn't quite hear what they were saying from outside the widow, but shortly after that a halo of golden magical dust swirled and twirled and rose up from the Bigfoot's mouth. It formed a ball of glittering stars. It was so shiny and sparkly that I was surprised the Bigfoot didn't wake from its slumber because of the sheer brilliance of the light.

They carefully maneuvered the ball into the container outside the window where it sat glowing like the lava in a mouth of an open volcano.

I know what you're thinking Bob. "You see magic all the time why was this so spectacular?" Honestly I couldn't tell you, but it was, and it was something I'll never forget. Perhaps it was because there was so much of it? Normally we only get a cupful of magic dust to sprinkle over us every day. But seeing this mound was like comparing a lightning bug to the sun. There was no comparison. Oh Bob! I can only hope that one day my flying and magical skills will be good enough to join the magic collectors... although I doubt it very much.

There was something else on our outing, however, which I found both fascinating and a little scary too. One of the other magic collectors collected dust from a child who appeared to be sleeping soundly. When the dust rose it was as black as night. It swished and swirled around the room violently, like it had a life of its own and wanted to hurt someone. I think it was the dust from a nightmare.

With the help of my mother, the magic collector trapped the dust and recited another incantation to make it disappear. I obviously didn't hear that one either, but it seemed to work and within a matter of seconds the black cloud poofed into nothingness.

Later that night I asked my mother why the other fairy had taken bad magic dust from the Bigfoot and she told me that "it's impossible to know what is inside the minds of these Bigfoots. It is usually only after we extract the dust that we find out". I'm not sure I could handle the nightmare dust like my mother had, but I at least wanted to try… someday … maybe. But in order to do that I have to go back to school. So, I guess there's nothing left to do but face the music.

Anxiously,
Petunia Pottersfield.

## Chapter 4 – Autumn's end

Dear Bob,

I am a little confused to say the least, and not for the reasons you might think. Things have been happening around town that just don't seem to quite add up. First of all, I did eventually return to school and, yes, it was a little awkward to begin with. But once I had told everyone that I had decided to stay away from potion making for a while, they all seemed to relax a little. I can't blame them really.

I suppose the first thing that surprised me this week was that I actually made a friend. Yes that's right, a real friend! Not a ladybug or a diary, no offence, but a real live fairy friend with arms and legs and everything. Her name is

Alisia Blossom and she is the nicest fairy I've ever met. She has long fiery red hair and wild lilac eyes. She's a little on the naughty side though, but I don't mind. I'm just happy that someone *wants* to be my friend.

Maybe that's why we get on so well; we're both forever getting into trouble, usually me by accident and her on purpose. I think that's why they always kept her in a different class to me too. Alisia is my age and has been going to my school all her life too, but I never met her before. I suppose Mrs. Scarrowtree figured that adding trouble with trouble would only give you mayhem, and thought it would be better if we never met. I don't think Mrs. Scarrowtree was expecting that I would become famous, or rather infamous, over my sludge monster and everyone would know my name.

That's why we met, you know, Bob. Alisia came up to me in the yard and congratulated me on my magnificent monster. I thought she was joking at first, or poking fun at me. But when I saw her very wide and cheeky grin, I knew she was genuinely please to meet a fellow troublemaker.

Alisia's father is one of the High Council Governors. That means that he's one of the fairies in charge of the workings of Furrow

Grove. I suppose Mr. Blossom would be like the boss co-ordinating all of the different fairy jobs making sure everything runs smoothly. Right now I'm sure he is busy ordering my father to hurry up with the re-stocking and my mother to fill the dust store to the brim.

The autumn fairy will soon hand over her job to the frost fairy. I don't know why it's the elemental fairies job to change the seasons of the year, but it is. The autumn fairy will tell the trees and plants it's time to sleep so that they won't get damaged by the frost when the frost fairy comes around. I suppose the frost fairies job is to ensure that everything stays asleep so that it can build up its energy for the coming of the spring fairy, who wakes them again. I don't suppose I need to tell you what the summer fairy does, now do I Bob?

I guess with all of her father's authority that perhaps Alisia is used to getting her own way and that's why she is a little bold. I reckon that's how she managed to get herself transferred into my class too, and I couldn't be happier about that.

I don't mind her wildness so much because she is also very generous. She gave me a handmade summer hat that she made out of daisy petals, and a beautiful purple pouch to carry you in, Bob. So now you can come with me everywhere. I've never had anyone just give me something before when it wasn't my birthday, and I will cherish them forever.

Amazingly, the hat fit perfectly. Finding a hat that will contain my giant mess of hair is normally done with great difficulty. But this one was just right.

Oh! But I don't want you to worry, Bob. I'm not going to stop writing just because I have a new friend. I think my mother was right when she told me that writing to you would be like having a friend to talk to and I have so much more to tell you. Stuff that I'm not sure I should burden my new friend with just yet. She might think I'm crazy and I don't want to scare her off.

It all began on the day of my brother's graduation. He received the highest marks in his class and the graduation ceremony took place just before he joined the F.P.A. My parents were very proud of him and my mother cried through the whole thing. I was proud of him too, but it made me wonder if my parents would ever cry with pride for me. So far, the only thing I've ever made them was disappointed.

We had a big party for Blackhawk and Alisia came over too. Oh it was great to have a friend over, Bob, and she was a welcome distraction from my brothers gloating over me. He called me names all day and Alisia told him to put a dung beetle in his mouth before she did. I laughed so hard that I think I might have actually farted—embarrassing, yes I know. I suppose I've never really had anyone stand up for me before and I didn't quite know how to react.

The next day Blackhawk started his first day of F.P.A. training and that's when everything changed. He became very quiet and reserved almost at once. He didn't shout at me or call me a name for three days and that's what got me worried. I wondered if it might have had something to do with Alisia's threat of a dung flavoured mouth, or if his military training had kicked in already. I know the F.P.A. training is excellent and I have heard of people becoming more disciplined over time, but one day is a bit quick for my liking.

Stranger still was the fact that he was actually *nice* to me, like a big brother should be. He said please and thank you to mother, and tidied his room until it shone in the sunshine. He even told me that he "loved me". Honestly,

I don't know exactly what's going on with him, but I think I like it.

That's not all though. Some of the other fairies around town have been acting a little strangely too. I know we're nearing our winter phase and everyone is getting a little tired, I suppose maybe a little more tired than usual because of the extra work they had to do this year because of me. But even still they are behaving very strangely indeed.

Yesterday as Alisia and I were walking to school we saw old man Duckweed. He was smiling from ear to ear and his black eyes were gleaming, like he had heard the best news in the world. He even did a little hop, kick, and a jump without the aid of his crooked walking stick. He dipped an imaginary hat in our direction, before carrying on with his happy dance all the way back to his putrid home. His behaviour seemed very odd to us both, but we kept on walking regardless.

When we got to school our teacher Mrs. Scarrowtree seemed sullen and withdrawn as well. She went through the motions of the lesson alright, but it seemed that her heart wasn't really in it. She didn't even bother to clad my classmates in their usual protective gear for potions that day. So, I decided it was safer if I stood in the background and just watched instead. I think everyone was quite relieved that I did.

Perhaps all this is some kind of pre-winter lull, but even the F.P.A. seemed somewhat sluggish recently. A blackbird flew into the middle of the fairy ring and it took them twice the usual time to arrive. And when they did, they all seemed somewhat apathetic towards the situation. They didn't bother to secure wayward fairies, instead they simply fired a pebble from a slingshot at the bird and it flew away.

I wonder does this happen to fairies sometimes? Maybe even *we* can get burned out eventually. But there were a lot of tired fairies out there, more than I ever remember seeing before. Perhaps that's just my imagination? Not to fear, the winter will be on us in two days and they will have all the time to rest then.

Confused,
Petunia Pottersfield.

## Chapter 5 – Mid-winter

Dear Bob

Well it's mid-winter and I have had the best and the worst six weeks of my life so far. You remember I told you about my new best friend Alisia? Well, it turns out that my new best friend gave me something along with the summer hat and purple bag. She also gave me the *purple itchies*.

The purple itchies is a nasty and highly contagious illness. It turns your whole body purple and makes you itch all over. I know she didn't mean to give it to me, but once our parents saw our skin starting to change colour we were both immediately isolated from the rest of the fairies. It wouldn't do to have every fairy in Furrow Grove spend their long winter rest scratching themselves into near insanity. I don't particularly want to be blamed for that one too.

Thankfully we were confined in a room together, otherwise I might have been bored to tears. We've spent the last six weeks talking, playing board games, and finding out more about each other. It turns out that Alisia's mother is a dust collector too. She and my mother have been working together for many years now. Who knew?

For the first four weeks we had a great time. We laughed, played games and stayed up late at night, although it's hard to tell *how* late when you're underground. All I know is that every night I *eventually* fell asleep, usually mid-sentence to Alisia, and I enjoyed every minute of it.

I suppose, I had been so thoroughly entertained by Alisia that I hadn't noticed the subtle changes in the tunnels. Normally all of the fairies would gather in the centre camber every night to dance and feast. It was wonderful to watch them through a half open door, even if we couldn't join in.

Day by day, however, it seemed to us that more and more fairies opted to stay home instead of joining the winter celebrations. This was very unusual behaviour for the fairies in winter, and it troubled me because fairies are not reclusive by nature.

Alisia and I began to think that the purple itchies had spread, regardless of our precautions. "Great we're going to be blamed for that too," Alisia had said.

I wasn't sure that it *was* the purple itchies though, because I had seen some of the missing fairies walking around the tunnels the next day and they didn't have a hint of a purple hue on their skin. So, when my mother came to deliver our meal that night I asked her if everything was okay.

"Oh, everything is fine," she had replied. "Don't worry, sweetheart. You two just concentrate on getting better."

But there was something behind her eyes, something about the way she furrowed her brow and pursed her lips into a thin line. There was something she wasn't telling me and I knew she was worried. But no matter how hard I pressed the subject, she didn't let on.

Alisia's mother didn't come to visit us that night and that set off even more alarm bells in our heads. The problem only seemed to get worse from then on. Eventually my father stopped visiting and when we peeked out of our door, the underground town was filled with the most despondent looking fairies that I had ever seen in my life.

Their lustrous skin was dull and grey, their eyes didn't sparkle and their wings hung limply behind them like they had been doused in water. The only person who looked like a happy fairy should was old man Duckweed, and that was more disconcerting than anything.

Alisia and I wondered if perhaps someone cast a spell on our fairy ring, giving each fairy an opposite personality. It would explain why everyone looked so depressed and why old man Duckweed was so overjoyed. Perhaps the spell had something to do with how he turned into a miserable old fairy in the first place. But why didn't it affect us?

Whatever the cause, I am beginning to get worried now, Bob. It's been nearly an entire day since anyone came to check on us. Our mothers and fathers seemed to have abandoned us completely and when we shout through the door, no one will answer us. They won't tell us what's going on or where our parents are. They just walk past us, like they're sleepwalking; their mouths opened and drooling, their eyes blank and staring.

Oh Bob, I do wonder what's going on and I hope everything *is* okay. Surely if there was something really the matter, my mother would have warned me or tried to get me out of here. Wouldn't she?

Our purple itchies are almost gone now. I know I should probably wait until someone tells me it's okay to leave isolation, but I'm too worried to stay in here. Alisia and I have decided that if no one comes for us tonight, we will have no choice but to leave the room and see for ourselves what's going on. Thankfully the door was never locked. But don't worry, Bob. I won't leave you here, I'll bring you with me.

Apprehensively,
Petunia Pottersfield.

## Chapter 6 – That night

Dear Bob,

Something is wrong. Something is terribly, terribly wrong. I am so scared and don't know what to do. But I think it's important to tell you everything so that if any other fairies find you, at least they'll know what has happened to us all.

Alisia and I are hiding at the moment; we were running for our lives. I don't know exactly what's gotten into everyone, but something wicked has affected the people of Furrow Grove. Whatever has changed them, they're in an awful hurry to do it to us too. It seems they've all lost their minds or something. It's like I'm in a nightmare world and I just can't wake up.

Once night came, and no one checked on us, Alisia and I crept out of our isolation room. At worst, I was expecting to just get into trouble when someone spotted us. But if there was some other illness spreading through the fairy ring, I also worried we might make it worse by infecting people with the purple itchies too. But we were left with little choice, and hunger made us braver.

When we came out, the tunnels were in complete darkness. No one had bothered to light the torches, which was a bad omen in itself. We thought it best to stay in the shadow in case a light might draw unwanted attention. I had no idea at the time just how right we were.

As we slunk through the empty chambers and desolate halls, we began to hear a sort of… chanting, I guess you'd call it. The words were dark, foreboding, and the ones we could make out were of someone being worship. It was a strange sound because fairies don't worship things. We are the balancers and caretakers of nature, and fairy law sees us as all equals. So to hear this chanting made my hairs stand on end.

I know the sound scared Alisia too because she thought it might be best just to return to our room and wait for someone else to help. But I couldn't just hang around and wait, I had to know what was going on. I couldn't just hide and leave my family to be hurt, or succumb to the myriad of other terrible things that conjured themselves in my mind. So I pressed onwards, convincing Alisia to follow me.

How stupid I was! I should have remembered that my ideas are never good ones. I should have listened to Alisia. If I had, then we might not be in the mess we are in right now. Oh Bob, what are we going to do?

We followed the chanting into a very deep chamber underground. It was one I'd never seen before… and I had spent many years wandering through the tunnels alone, so I knew them well. The chamber wasn't flanked on every side with the mushroom root like the other tunnels. Instead, it looked as though someone had dug a hole in one of the walls and created a separate chamber directly into the ground. Dirt crumbled and fell from the haphazardly hewn walls and a network of tree roots held up the ceiling.

From the ledge high up in the chamber, we saw that it was filled with every single Furrow Grove fairy. They all looked as terrible as each other; drawn, pale, and swaying slightly in unified misery. A hoard of half-living beings who were once people we knew and loved.

I wanted to cry, I wanted to crumble when I saw them because it was then I knew things were far worse than we first thought.

As we got closer I recognised one of the voices that shouted above the hum of melancholy whispering. It echoed and hissed like a howling winter breeze, and the words froze my very soul. It was old man Duckweed. He stood at the head of the chamber on a raised platform of stones. The stones were arranged in a spiralling pattern which climbed higher and higher until old man Duckweed towered over the crowd.

"This is the just first phase, my people," he said. "With careful planning I have managed to secure Furrow Grove, and soon I will branch out into *all* of the other fairy rings known to us. Together, we will rise up and enslave the non-magical creatures of this world. Too long have we let them enjoy domination over us. Why should we be the ones to live in the dirt? Why should we scrimp for measly winter rations, when they grow fat from our labours? Why should we fear them because they are bigger than us? With the combined forces of our people it will soon be *them* who fear us."

I couldn't believe my ears, Bob. I was fully sure that someone amongst the crowd would shout at him and tell him to stop being such a goblin. But there were no objections. Not one! Instead the crowd cheered and the thunderous roar nearly made me lose my footing. Thankfully Alisia caught me just before I went tumbling right into the middle of the gathering. Honestly, what would I do without her?

But I'm so confused, Bob. I don't know what's happening to everyone. What's worse is that when Alisia and I edged closer to the crowd, I saw my parents and Blackhawk in the middle of them all. They were as pious and waxen looking as the rest. They cheered on Duckweed, like he had been elected owner of all the Universe, or something.

How could they cheer on such a hateful and dangerous plan? What had happened to change everyone's normally cautious approach to all things outside of Furrow Grove? To use our magic to oppress or harm another living being would break the most sacred rule we fairies have. They all know that, but yet, there they were… willing and able. Oh Bob, what has happened to everyone and how do I fix it?

In the midst of my despair my clumsy foot managed to dislodge loose rocks from our hiding place, and sent them tumbling. It would have been fortunate if the crowd were cheering at the time, but you and I both know that I do *not* have that kind of luck. It just so happened that, right at that particular moment, a lull came over the crowd.

The rocks bumped and banged all the way down the quiet cavern wall, dislodging more dirt and larger stones. It sounded like a blacksmith hammering in the dead silence of the night. Bob, it couldn't have made any more noise if it tried.

That's when they all looked up and saw us. I think Alisia was still hopeful that the sea of menacing eyes was friendly in some way. She waved with an awkward chuckle. Utter silence followed our discovery for about two seconds, but it seemed more like twenty minutes as we waited for their response. We should have just run for it when we had the chance.

"Get them!" Duckweed shouted, closely followed by a crashing of heavy footsteps heading in our direction.

Alisia and I got to our feet as quickly as we could and ran through the corridors in terror. We didn't know what they were going to do to us if they caught us. But by the looks in their dull lifeless eyes, it wasn't a going to be good.

We ran and ran until our lungs hurt and our hearts pounded in our ears. At one point we were both so blinded by our terror that we lost track of one another. Oh Bob, that was the last thing I wanted to happen. Whatever was going on around us I didn't want to face it alone—and I suspected neither did Alisia.

I dodged left and right as the crowd pursued me though the corridors. Their hands grabbed for me, some of them managing to catch the ends of my hair. I screamed and pushed my tired legs to run faster. The one and only thing I had in my favour was the corridors were too narrow to fly. Given my penchant for flying into things instead of around them, I don't think I would have gotten very far. But by some miracle, my legs did an amazing job and I was able to pull away and hide in a small chamber, unseen, as they thundered past.

I couldn't breathe, Bob. My head swam and my body ached and I cried in deep, sobbing, hiccups. But I knew I couldn't stay there. Once they realised I was no longer ahead of them, they'd be back.

With the back of my hand I wiped the tears away and set my jaw. I had to find Alisia. I had to get us both out of here. Peering out of the door, I was relieved to see the coast was clear. As quietly as I could I crept out into the root tunnels again and began my stealthy search for my only friend.

Thankfully we found each other again before the mob did. Alisia managed to out run them too, but just barely. Her clothes were ripped and she had a nasty scratch on her arm. I hugged her as tightly as I could and she shuddered against me as she cried silently. We had to hide, find some place the others wouldn't look.

From a perch well out of their line of sight, I watched them skulk between the tunnels like ghosts. The only place they seemed to avoid was the main fairy dust chamber, although I had no idea why. Regardless, it seemed like the best place to hide so we could come up with a plan.

Together we snuck through the shadows. When we were only a few steps away, I heard one of the other fairies shout that he'd seen us. There was a commotion and the sound of pursuit came toward us. My heart took off in a gallop and I grabbed Alisia's hand, running full pelt into the chamber. We dove into the golden sand, burring ourselves in the shiny silt.

I think I must have held my breath until I was blue in the face. The magic from the dust tingled my skin and didn't help matters. Alisia, on the other hand, was gasping loudly and choking on the dust. I held my hand over her mouth until the last footsteps dissolved into the distance. Even then, we stayed frozen, unable to move, unable to speak, unable to do anything but wait for our luck to run out.

Once the mob passed by, and silence returned, I noticed something odd. The fairy dust reserves we were sitting in, were full. Normally by this time in our hibernation it would be half empty. It's our life force and every fairy must have at least one scoop a day to stay fit and healthy. Up until yesterday Alisia and I had gotten ours regularly. By the looks of things it seemed that perhaps we were only ones. Maybe that's why they're all acting strangely? But why would they stop taking it?

Eventually the others were gone long enough that I relaxed a little. I tried to speak, to come up with a plan, but I had nothing. All I could do was look at Alisia and she at me. I can feel her still shaking as I write now. What do I do, Bob?

Oh no! I hear them coming again… I have to stop writing now… I'm so scared.

Terrified,
Petunia Pottersfield.

## Chapter 7 – A few moments later

Dear Bob,

The worst has happened and I'm so cold. Bob, I can't stop crying and I am absolutely terrified and alone right now. They've got Alisia. They've got her! I can barely write because I'm crying so much. It was so scary, and it was *my* parents who caught her. Worst of all, it was completely *my* fault again.

I have never seen such an evil and twisted look in my parent's eyes before. My heart is aching for both her and my family, but at least I know what has happened now. At least I know that they couldn't help it.

Let me tell you before my fingers become too numb.

As we lay beneath the fairy dust I heard footsteps coming into the room. It was closely followed by snarls and the strangely altered voices of my family. It was as if all the sweetness and love had been sucked out of their voice, leaving only a harsh and rasping sound behind. I saw my mother flying above us, but for some reason, while we were in the fairy dust, she couldn't see me.

Stupidly, I thought that if only I could only reach out and hug her she would remember me, she would remember how it used to be, and everything would go back to being normal. How could I have been so foolish? Stupid, stupid, stupid!

That's when I made the *next* biggest mistake of my life. I reached out my hand to try and catch hold of my mother's shoe. I heard Alisia scream "No!", but I kept my hand out because I couldn't believe that any magic was more powerful than my love for my mother.

My mother saw me, and I saw the deadly and uncaring look in her eyes. I realised my mistake then, Bob, but I froze. I couldn't move. Just as she swooped down to grab hold of my wrist and yank me into the air, Alisia jumped up from the dust and pushed me back down into it.

As I lay there half buried in the golden sprinkles, I watched my mother toss Alisia towards my father and Blackhawk. They grabbed hold of her legs and arms to stop her struggling.

"Run!" she had shouted at me. "Run and get some help Petunia. Hurry!"

And I did.

I ran as fast as my little legs could carry me, but it never seemed quite fast enough. I dashed and ducked, dived and weaved, and hid in the smallest place that I could find until eventually, I lost my pursuers. And that's where I stayed for the longest time. I didn't dare breathe too loudly or shift my feet too much in case someone heard me.

I felt so bad, Bob. It was my fault again. I was the one who got Alisia caught and I worried about what they were going to do to her. I had to find out, Bob. I just had to.

So, once the coast seemed clear I came out of my hiding place. I kept to the smaller, darker tunnels and made my way back toward Duckweed's chamber below ground. Once or twice a mindless fairy would shuffle past in one of the larger tunnels and I would nearly get caught. But I held my breath and quietened my heartbeat as best as I could and hugged the shadowy walls. With much trepidation, I finally made it down into the chamber.

Most of the fairies had gathered again after my little interruption, and still standing on his large circular platform, was old man

Duckweed. As I hunkered in an obscure corner I heard screaming and shouting coming from the chamber below. It was Alisia being dragged towards the platform.

I wanted to scream "let her go!" I wanted to fly down and grab her out of their cruel grasp. How I wished I could create another slime monster now. I wanted to cast some kind of spell that would release her. But I couldn't… I daren't. Everything I had done so far had only ever made things worse, so I stayed where I was and just watched with tears streaming down my face.

"Where is the other one?" Duckweed roared, but the mindless zombies didn't answer.

He seemed stronger and more foreboding since the last time I saw him in the streets. His usual scraggly beard was fuller and he no longer used his crooked waking stick for walking. Instead, he banged it on the stone beneath his feet like a staff that commanded his mindless minions. The sound boomed in the air and it made me jump.

I remember asking myself, "how did this wiry old man manage to turn the entire fairy ring into his willing followers?" It seemed almost impossible to me. Most of us would have rather run headfirst into a bee hive before we'd listen to this wretched old fairy. *So how did he do it?* I was about to get my answer, and it was nothing short of pure evil.

As Alisia was dragged toward Duckweed, her fiery red hair flailing about only in a slightly wilder fashion than her arms and legs, I watched as he waved his staff over the platform. Suddenly, the grey centre stone in the ground beneath him began to open up. It slid with a thunderous rumble across the floor to reveal a small hidden compartment below. The hole was filled with something I recognised very well and it sent a shiver through my body, making my blood run cold.

It was black nightmare dust!

Somehow, somewhere, this old gremlin had managed to get hold of an enormous amount of the nightmare dust. It gleamed, shimmered, and moved like black lava trying to rise up from a volcano. I swear, Bob, I could almost hear it hiss and curse as it did. I watched as old man Duckweed dipped the head of his crooked staff into the vile pit of darkness, and then point it at Alisia.

Without warning, a black snaking shot of electricity flew from the tip of his staff and it hit Alisia square in her stomach. She let out a scream and it took everything that I had to restrain myself. I watched in terror as her face slowly became ashen grey and all life drain from her eyes. She stopped fighting the fairies carrying her and eventually stood motionless amongst them in a sea of vacant expressions.

Alisia was lost and I knew it. I was alone, utterly alone now, and it was all up to *me* to help everyone. *Me,* Bob, *me!* We're all doomed.

It was then that I realised old man Duckweed must have been planning this for a long time. I remembered seeing him shooting the same type of spark at the larger fairies whom he told to "go on a diet". He didn't care about their weight at all, did he? He was only practicing his aim. He must have learned how to syphon magic dust and hoarded only nightmare dust.

Of course, it made sense that he would have begun with the F.P.A. that's why my brother changed so quickly. They must have been the first ones hit, otherwise they would have noticed a change in the fairies around them.

With the F.P.A. out of the way, he would have a clear path to do as he pleased. But why? Why did he want to raise an army? Why did he want to scare away the Bigfoots? I didn't hang around to find out.

With a steely resolve to not doom us all, I slunk through the tunnels and headed up toward the surface. There was no one left in Furrow Grove who hadn't been turned so I had to leave. I was the last one, and everyone was depending on me to save them. The thought made my stomach churn, but I carried on climbing regardless.

I had to leave the fairy ring to get help. I'd have to suffer the consequences of frost bitten wings and find a neighbouring fairy ring. I didn't know where to look. But what I *did* know was that Duckweed's army wouldn't surface from Furrow Grove until the frost fairy had finished her work. This gave me about three weeks to find help. Surely I could at least do that, right?

I wasn't certain another fairy village would let me in even if I did find one. You see, Bob, fairies are very territorial. Each ring has a certain amount of area they cover and woe-betide the fairy that enters into another's territory. I'm not sure why that is, but as a result the Elders thought it best to not teach the children the location of other villages. So, I had no idea where the nearest one was. Regardless, I took off into the freezing night to try, at least. After all, who *else* could I get help from?

But it wasn't long before the frost stiffened my wings and I was forced to walk. Now, as I write to you, I am at the end of my energy. It's so cold and walking in the frozen grass is exhausting. Not to mention dangerous. Three times, so far, a field mouse has tried to drag me into its burrow, and I suspect it wasn't to warm me. I managed to get away, but only just barely.

I'm so tired, Bob. I'm so cold. But I have to keep going. I'm the only one who can raise the alarm and save my family, Alisia, and my town too. I only hope that luck will finally side with me on this most important mission, and lead me to someone who *can* help—anyone but me.

Frozen and alone,
Petunia Pottersfield.

## Chapter 8 – Near Winter's End

Dear Bob,

Why is it me who is always on the bad side of Lady Luck? I honestly think I might have offended her in a past life, or something, and now she is getting her revenge on me. Things I'm afraid have gone from bad to worse. "How is that even possible?" I hear you ask. Well, this is *me* you're talking about here.

After I last wrote I'm afraid I didn't manage to find another fairy ring. In fact, I'm fully sure that I was circling around Furrow Grove for hours. It wasn't long before I succumbed to the cold and I passed out amongst the weeds. I don't remember much of what happened next, but I do faintly remember hearing thunderously heavy footsteps coming closer, and closer. My blood ran as cold as the frost around me when I heard it, because I knew what it was, Bob. It was a Bigfoot. It couldn't have been anything else because it was just so loud and clumsy.

The thought of getting squashed beneath its giant boot was enough for me to scramble, half-coherently, beneath a rock. That's where I fell into blackness again. My next memory was of a warm, sweet breath blowing a gale over my body. When I looked up, I saw two enormous blue eyes, framed in a mop of golden hair, peering back at me.

The Bigfoot had seen me and had cupped me in her gigantic hands. I tried to scream, but nothing came out. I don't remember if I passed out again because of the cold or the fright, but I did.

I was woken next by warm sunshine covering me from head to toe, like a cosy blanket of light. Oh it was wonderful, Bob, to finally be out of the freezing cold. For a moment I had actually forgotten the horrible events of in Furrow Grove and my semiconscious nightmare.

As I yawned and stretched, my hand hit something solid. I jumped up quickly and the memories came flooding back to me all at once in a blinding flash of panic. I didn't know where I was or what was going on, but every direction I tried to run I was met with the same invisible force field. I tried to fly straight up, but a strange metal roof, with holes poked in it, stopped me. I realised then that it was a massive jar of some kind, and the lid was fastened on too tight for me to open. No matter how hard I pushed or kicked at my surroundings, I couldn't get out. I was trapped, and that's when I saw her.

Sitting in the centre of an enormous room was a Bigfoot. She was surrounded by colossal toys of every description and was busily combing the hair of a doll about three times my size. She wasn't the biggest Bigfoot I had ever seen, but she was big enough to make me gasp in fright.

She must have heard me because at that moment she looked over and got up with an excited hop. She trundled awkwardly over the wooden floor, tripping over her own foot in the excitement. Her footsteps were so loud and heavy that I thought the jar might fall from its perch and come crashing down to the floor. Unfortunately for me it didn't, and in no time at all she had her warm sticky hands wrapped around the glass.

"Hello little fairwy," she said with an excited look in her giant eyes.

I didn't answer and not just because it was forbidden to talk to a Bigfoot, I was just too frightened to speak.

"Hello little fairwy," she said again more crossly.

This time, when I didn't answer, she shook the jar I was in and sent me crashing into its sides.

"Stop it," I yelled back.

I didn't mean to yell, but her clumsy hands were in danger of shaking my brains out. She stopped, held the jar in place, and watched me for a moment. Her eyes started to well up and tears the size of my head rolled down her cheeks. I realised then that she must have only been a very young child. I had obviously upset her and the last thing I needed right now was an upset Bigfoot.

I knew that I was lucky in a way, because she didn't seem interested in dissecting me… at the moment. Rather she wanted to play with me instead. If I talked to her, played with her, she might tell the larger Bigfoots about me and *they* might not be so friendly. I suspected that even if I *did* talk to her, no adult Bigfoot would believe her story about fairies. They'd have to see me first, and I fully intended on escaping before then.

I had no time for playing. I had to help my family, my friend, everyone, and time was wasting away. I had to get this Bigfoot child to help, somehow.

"I'm sorry," I said to her in the gentlest voice I could manage. "You scared me, that's all. My name is Petunia Potterfield. What's yours?"

"Elizabeth," she replied, sniffling and wiping the tears from her face.

"It's very nice to meet you, Elizabeth," I replied. "But could you tell me where I am?"

"You're in my woom."

Elizabeth then proceeded to lift my jar and whirl it around the room. I've never felt so dizzy in all of my life, Bob. I swear I nearly threw up all over the jar. She introduced me to all of her toys in succession and decided that I simply *must* have a tea party with them.

"Oh, I'd love to," I replied "but I can't drink tea if I'm in this jar, now can I?"

She didn't fall for it. These Bigfoots are smarter then they look.

"If I let you out you'll just fly away."

"Oh, but I promise I won't," I said. Even *I* didn't believe me then.

"No. It's only pwetend tea anyway. So you don't weally need to dwink it."

The logic of this Bigfoot child was infuriating. I didn't have time to coax her into letting me out of the jar, nor did I have the patience. But I had no choice. I had to play it cool and somehow get out of this mess so I could help Furrow Grove. Winter will be over soon and the spring fairy would begin the thaw. Once that happened, old man Duckweed would be free to spread his evil plan and all hope would be lost.

I decided then that perhaps I could use my misfortune to my benefit. This Elizabeth had big legs and could bound around the nearby fields much quicker than I could fly. She was also tall enough that I would be able to spot a fairy ring from her shoulder and keep warm in her pockets. If I wanted her help though, I knew that I would have to tell her about old man Duckweed… about Furrow Grove. Children always know when you are telling the truth and I had to get her to trust me.

"Elizabeth," I started, looking sternly into her eyes. "Something very bad has happened and I need your help."

"What's happened?" she replied in a whisper, her eyes wide.

I knew that "bad things" in a young child's mind was something that couldn't be left untackled. I was using her childish sense of justice against her and I knew it. Did I think I was doing the right thing? I never do, but I had to make her understand and feel the urgency of my plight.

"Oh, I don't know if I should tell you. It might scare a young girl like you."

"Hum," she huffed "I'm six yearws old now. I'm a big girwl and I'm not scarwed of anything."

With her determination and defiance brewed up, I told the young Bigfoot about everything that happened. Her eyes grew so wide that I thought they might actually pop out of her head. Surprisingly, they didn't and she remained calm. Perhaps these Bigfoots aren't so bad after all.

I made her promise never to tell anyone about me, or the fairy ring. I told her that if she wanted to be friends with us afterward, she must keep it a secret—otherwise we would have to move away.

I think she bought it, Bob.

I don't like lying, especially not to little children… even if they are ginormous. Maybe I *will* come back some day. Maybe we *will* become friends, and then it won't be a lie. That is, if old man Duckweed doesn't turn me into a fairy zombie first.

For now, though, she has agreed to help me. But it will have to wait until morning. Her parents said it was getting too late to go for a walk. She has hidden me away from their prying eyes and under her bed amongst the dust and forgotten toys. Time is running out, Bob. I can just barely make out the Bigfoots window from under the bed and the frost fairy seems to be tiring. The delicate patterns of frozen art are taking nearly all night to form on the window now. I only hope that she can hold out, just a little bit longer.

Hopefully,
Petunia Pottersfield.

## Chapter 9 – Winter's End

Dear Bob,

Good news and bad news! The good news is that after nearly a week of searching, Elizabeth and I found another fairy ring. She let me free and I promised to return to her once I had gotten rid of the "Bad Man". I fully intend on keeping that promise.

Turns out that the Bigfoots call themselves humans, and, for a human, I found Elizabeth to be a very sweet and kind-hearted girl. You never know, it could be the start of something great. Perhaps a new chapter in the relationship between humans and fairies? I can only imagine what Mr. Tumbleseed would think of that; his enthusiasm for all things outside the fairy ring would see him go slightly gaga.

The bad news, however, proved to be more devastating than I could have imagined. After Elizabeth tip-toed away from the new fairy ring (for fear her footsteps would set off alarms) I found my way into the tunnels of a village called Sapling Corm. It was very similar to Furrow Grove. All of the tunnels seemed to have the same layout. So it was easy for me to find my way to the central chamber, where I expected they would all be singing, dancing, and making merriment.

It had been some time since I saw fairies enjoying the winter like this, and it warmed my heart to hear familiar songs of Wintertide. I can't honestly say that they were as pleased to see me though. I was immediately recognised as an outsider, largely due to my red clothing, and in an instant a swarm of fairies in green and F.P.A. officers surrounded me.

They shouted things like "throw her in the dungeon," and "banish her to the frost," even before I had a chance to speak. I stuttered and stumbled words out, but they were drowned in the incensed voices of Sapling Corm's residence. I'm telling you, Bob, I never knew that fairy hospitality left so much to be desired. I was sure they were going to hurt me.

That's when the flying F.P.A. grabbed hold of my arms and lifted me clean off my feet and into the air. I think it was kind of them in a way, because the crowd down below were all but ready to get out their pitch forks and chase me back out into the cold.

I was then unceremoniously dumped in a room which resembled Furrow Grove's council chamber. Along the curved tunnel walls were elegant paintings of tall Sapling Corm dignitaries. Each one of them scowled at me terribly while their noses were held in the air. Ahead of me, a large smooth wooden table and five seats were perched on top of a raised platform.

Suddenly, the large doors behind me opened and Elder fairies, dressed in dark green clothing, silently filled into the rows of benches behind me. They stared at me with such hatred and anger that I had to try very hard not to cry at that point. Like a funeral procession, five more Elders solemnly strode in and sat in the tall chairs in front of me, all the while trying to turn me to ice with their eyes. I knew that if my parents could see me now, they would hang their heads in embarrassment yet again.

There I was, making another catastrophic mistake and it made me wonder. Why am I so stupid, Bob? I know that entering a neighbouring fairy ring is forbidden, so why couldn't I think of any other way to help Furrow Grove? Surely I could have talked

Elizabeth into reaching down and grabbing old man Duckweed by his stinky black robe and tossing him into the next county. But what would I do about the zombie fairies then?

It was no use thinking about what I should have done at that point. As my father used to say "mistakes makes us better at making better choices in the future". I honestly don't know if that's true, but I've always hoped that it was.

The angry whispers hushed into silence as the five council Elders slowly lowered themselves onto their chairs. They each wore tall green and golden hats, which sat on top of their head like a rooster's cockscomb, and stately robes of the same colour which had glided behind them like a peacock's tail.

To say that I was intimidated was an understatement of the highest order. I could feel my knees knocking and almost give way as I stood in front of the grand table of dignitaries.

"This trail will come to order," the rather large fairy in the centre said.

His red, puffy face and piercing blue eyes gave me the impression that he was in no mood for a trial. But his demeanour was one of propriety and grandiosity. The expressions on the four other council members didn't differ much either.

He banged his gavel heavily on the table and the noise made me jump. This man was clad robes that seemed to glitter with more gold than the others.

"What is your name fairy and where do you come from?" he questioned.

"P-Petunia Pottersfield from Furrow Grove, Sir," I answered with a dry throat.

"Petunia Pottersfield of Furrow Grove, you are hereby charged with the unlawful entry into Sapling Corm. How do you plead?"

"Please, Sir. Something terrible has happened and …"

"How do you plead, guilty or not guilty?" he roared at me.

"It's true. I am obviously here so I am obviously guilty," I answered with resignation.

The angry whispers rose up from behind me like the waves of the sea, growing ever louder. He banged his gavel once again and silenced the spectators.

"I can see that you are a young fairy. Perhaps you did not know it is a crime to trespass into a neighbouring fairy ring. Is this the case?"

"No, Sir. I know that I shouldn't have come here."

I could see his face getting redder and redder as I answered his questions. I only hoped that he would, at least, hear me out at some point.

"Do you know why it is a crime and what the punishment is?"

"No, Sir. I'm afraid I don't."

With an exasperated sigh, and a curse at Furrow Grove's poor education system, he proceeded to tell me why they were all so angry with me. Oh, Bob, if I had any idea I might have thought twice about coming here.

He told me, in a flurry of eccentric hand movements and over flamboyant words (some of which I didn't understand), that many thousands of years ago, bad weather and the greedy hand of the Bigfoots had brought hardship to the fairy world. Food was scarce and many fairies resorted to stealing the hard earned forages of other fairy rings. War broke out and many fairies lost their lives.

It was a horrific time in our past, one that they had vowed never to repeat. A law was created that forbids fairies from even entering another's territory, never mind entering their fairy ring. It seems that this is also why we wear different colours, so a trespasser can be seen easily.

The punishment for breaking this law was the harshest punishment that any fairy could ever receive. If he or she was found guilty of breaking this law, they would have their wings clipped. Oh Bob, I got so scared that I cried right in front of the entire council. Some hero I was.

To have your wings clipped meant that you would never fly again. What is a fairy if she cannot fly? I would be alone and jobless for the rest of my life, shunned even more than I am right now. It was all too much for me and I couldn't stop myself from crying.

I think that perhaps the large council member felt sorry for me, because his eyes became softer as I desperately pleaded with him not to clip my wings. His voice became quieter and he asked me to explain to him why I had entered Sapling Corm. I was grateful for his patience as I spluttered out my tale through tears, sobs, and yes I'll admit it, a snotty nose.

I told them of the changes in my family and the other fairies. I told them about how Alisia was captured and what old man Duckweed had done to her. I told them of his plans for Furrow Grove, and every other fairy ring in the area.

His eyes widened as I spun my tale and his red face grew a ghostly shade of white, as did the others. After taking a few moments, to let the tale settle in, he turned to his council members before banging his gavel once more.

"This trial will be adjourned until a later time. We must consider what Petunia Pottersfield of Furrow Grove has told us and come to a unanimous decision. In the meantime, Ms. Pottersfield, you will be taken to the F.P.A. headquarters where you will await our decision."

And this is where I am now, Bob. I am lying on a lumpy mattress in a cold cell of the F.P.A.'s headquarters, waiting to see what they will do to me. I am so scared, Bob. I don't know what to do or what else I can say to them to make them understand. How can I convince them that I didn't mean to break the laws? All I wanted was to help my village, and now, not only have I let them down, but I might very well lose my wings over it too.

I wish you could talk, Bob. I wish you could tell me that everything will be okay. But I know you can't. All that's left to do now is to curl up on the cold bed in my tiny cell and pretend to be in my old room… remembering the warmth of my mother's hugs.

Tearfully,

Petunia Pottersfield.

.

## Chapter 10 – That night

Dear Bob,

Well, I still have my wings… but only just barely. The large council member, who I later found out was a man named Mr. Ruddy, agreed to spare me that much. He said it wasn't my fault because I obviously wasn't made aware of the penalty for crossing a territory. It should, by right, be my teachers who should be blamed.

I'm not sure that my teachers would agree. I think most of their time was occupied with trying not to get me, or one of the other children, killed. But I said nothing about it. I didn't want to get into any more trouble. As it was, I could feel the fickle grip of Lady Luck slipping away.

Mr. Ruddy sort of blurted out the worst part of his news; that no one in Sapling Corm could help me. I could see he was flustered and somewhat abashed as he explained why. If he allowed them to go to Furrow Grove, then they would be in violation of the same law. And even though this was an emergency, he couldn't justify putting his fairies in danger.

I was devastated when he told me, Bob. I protested, pleaded, begged, for his help… he refused with a wobble of his jowls and a deep scowl. It was no use, he had made up his mind. Honestly, I didn't know where to turn or what to do next. If *he* wasn't going to help me, then there was no other help that I could think of. My heart nearly broke in two as I pictured what would happen to everyone I left behind.

Thankfully, the clever (and somewhat eccentric) Mr. Ruddy had a plan. I'm glad that Furrow Grove don't have to depend entirely on me, otherwise they would have been lost to the nightmare dust and evil old man Duckweed. But what I didn't realise at the time, Bob, was that Mr. Ruddys' plan was something I *would* have to carry out entirely on my own.

Furrow Grove is doomed, Bob. *Doomed* I tell you.

His plan began with me learning how to syphon fairy dust from dreams. Mr. Ruddy told me that fairy dust can be syphoned from everything, including fairies. The plan was to sneak back into Furrow Grove during the sleeping hours, syphon the nightmare dust from their bodies, and free them from their living nightmare. And I was to do this entirely on, my, own.

"Are you kidding me?" I hear you scream, because I screamed it too.

Here I am, the "jinx" of Furrow Grove charged with syphoning out not just one ball of nightmare dust, but hundreds all at the same time… and with no one else to help me.

I stuttered and mumbled and gestured wildly at Mr. Ruddy trying to explain to him that I couldn't do it. I remembered my mother and another dust collector having difficulty controlling just one nightmare, so how was I supposed to manage that many on my own? I couldn't even brew a simple potion without its contents trying to devour my classmates.

I told him everything then. I told him how I wasn't able to use my magic properly, how I couldn't even fly in a straight line, and I begged him to send someone, anyone, to help me. But he refused and I lost all hope in that moment. I can't tell you in words how fast my heart sank into my boots. Even if I *did* try to carry out his plan I was sure that I would only have made things worse… somehow.

That's when Mr. Ruddy sat me down in my cell and told me something which gave me a glimmer of hope. He told me a story about a young fairy in his village that was just like me, maybe even a little worse. Jacinto was his name, and many years ago Sapling Corm was nearly taken out of existence on several occasions by his calamities.

One day, however, a Bigfoot discovered their fairy ring and held many of them captive. Turns out that this Jacinto boy's powers were just too strong to be held safely in a classroom, and that's why he couldn't control them. As soon as Jacinto decided to help his fellow fairies and opened all of his powers to their fullest, he quickly realised that he was the most powerful fairy who had ever existed. He defeated the Bigfoot and saved his town from disaster.

Mr. Ruddy told me then that I reminded him a lot of Jacinto. He believes that I have the same kind of power inside of me and that all I had to do was to believe in myself. All I had to do was to trust that I could do it, and it will happen. I don't know if he's right, but it gave me hope that perhaps if someone like Jacinto could save his fairy ring, then maybe I could too.

But first things first, Mr. Ruddy and I have to summon the frost fairy.

Optimistically,
Petunia Pottersfield.

## Chapter 11 – Extended Winter

Dear Bob,

At the setting of the sun Mr. Ruddy, the council members, and I braved the cold hard surface of above ground to summon the frost fairy. You see, Bob, elemental fairies only work at night. They don't live in fairy rings like us either. I'm not actually quite sure where they live, but they don't often drop around for a cup of tea, if you catch my drift. That's why they have to be summoned.

An elemental fairy is the most powerful fairy known in existence. They can also be somewhat temperamental and so you had better have, not just a good reason for calling them from their duties, but a *great* reason when you do. Mr. Ruddy warned me of the consequences one could suffer… and it would curl your toes to hear it.

I can't imagine what it might be like as an elemental fairy. It must be difficult really. Elementals are the only fairies who roam freely in the outside world. Some say that they have so much magic inside of them that they are completely invisible to those who don't use or believe in it. That's probably why the humans haven't ever caught one.

Working in the dark of night must also be quite difficult. For the autumn fairy to have to fly around and touch each leaf and flower individually and turn the seasons, must be exhausting. I can understand why it takes the autumn fairy a couple of attempts to get *all* of the leaves on a tree to turn. The darkness must make it difficult to spot them all and that's probably why some of leaves remain green. I imagine it would be like trying to switch on a billion stars all at the same time.

However they work and wherever they lived, at that particular moment, was only something I pondered on to pass the time. I was about to meet the frost fairy for the very first time in my short life, and I was excited. It's not often a regular fairy gets to meet someone so important. You'd think Mr. Ruddy's tales would have made me scared of her... but this is *me* we're talking about.

I was sure that she would be able to help me. As she didn't live in a fairy ring, she wouldn't be subject to the same laws as the rest of us. I hoped she wouldn't refuse on such an important matter. Winter was almost done now anyway, so she must be looking for something else to do, surely?

The council members gathered in a small circle in the centre of what was left of their village. The frost had killed their old houses leaving nothing but a circular mound on the ground, as it had done in Furrow Grove. I didn't feel sorry for the old houses though, because I knew it wouldn't be long before they sprouted to life. Then they would be filled with the sounds of excited fairies again… well, at least I hoped they would.

Mr. Ruddy began the chant to summon the frost fairy. He took hold of the others council member's hands and, in a whispering echo, they repeated his words. They didn't do so in unison though, Bob. It was like listening to an echo of an echo. Each member waited for a count of three words before reciting the chant. It was quite beautiful to hear really, although I had no idea what they were saying.

A flurry of jumbled words filled my ears and indeed the night sky too. It was as if they were speaking a different, more ancient, language which made no sense to me at all.

Without warning, they all stopped and everything became quiet once again. Someway off in the distance I heard the eerie hoot of an owl and it broke the silence, but only momentarily.

We waited there for longer than my wings were comfortable with, and it almost seemed like nothing was going to happen.

"There," one of the council members said pointing to the sky.

When I looked up I didn't see anything at first, but eventually something shiny caught my eye. Way off in the distance, and nestled between the bright stars, a faint light started to move amongst them. It floated as gently as a snowflake tumbling through the air, while at the same time it twinkled like ice in the morning sun. As it came closer it started to take the shape of the most beautiful fairy I had ever seen.

Bob, I nearly lost my breath altogether. Her wings sparkled like star dust and her dress was made out of the softest snow. Her hair was pure white, and her eyes were as blue and clear as the morning sky. She floated elegantly down toward us leaving a trail of sparkling winter dust floated behind her. It coated everything in its path in a delicate layer of frost.

Oh Bob, it was like something out of a most magical dream.

I was speechless when she landed. I couldn't even mutter an awkward "hello." I didn't have to though. Thankfully, Mr. Ruddy did all of the talking for me. He explained everything to her, in length, and the dangers that we all faced. She silently listened, keeping her snow white hands gently clasped in front of her.

When Mr. Ruddy finished the tale I expected to hear her gasp in horror, but she didn't. She didn't move her lips or make any gestures at all. She stood there like a frozen statue and it made me cross. Mr. Ruddy didn't say anything else either. They simply looked at each other with little more than a silent nod between the both of them.

"Well?" I blurted out, expecting some kind of answer.

"Hush, child," replied Mr. Ruddy, raising a finger but keeping his eyes firmly locked on the frost fairy.

That made me even crosser. I wanted to stomp my feet and demand that someone say or do something. I had wasted enough time trying to convince Elizabeth, then Mr. Ruddy, and now the frost fairy, that someone needed to help my family and my town. Frustration bubbled up inside of me and I just couldn't keep it in anymore. Bob, I just couldn't.

"I will *not* hush," I said, just a little too loudly. "I mean no disrespect, but time is running out and someone needs to do *something*. Please, I need your help frost fairy. Please help me."

My request was honest and urgent, but she carried on looking at Mr. Ruddy without so much as a sideways glance in my direction. It was Mr. Ruddy who answered my desperate pleas.

"You would do well to trust others more," he said. "Winter is silent, it is slow and contemplative. It does not rush like spring or wilt like autumn, nor is it flamboyant and loud like summer. The frost fairy is like winter, and will consider her options carefully and quietly. You assume that everything works like you and I, Petunia. But it doesn't. The frost fairy speaks to me in my mind. Her thoughts are as clear and transparent as the ice she creates, but they are as sharp as them too. Have patience, young fairy."

I never knew this and my ignorance made my face flush bright red. Of course she wouldn't just stand there and say nothing, would she Bob? How stupid I had been, yet again. I tell you Bob from that moment on I stood silently and humbly and daren't utter another word as the two fairies continued their silent conversation.

It took some time, but eventually the frost fairy turned her azure eyes toward me. I was transfixed on their purity. There wasn't a fleck or a hint of another colour in them, and I couldn't look away. Somewhere in the background I was aware that Mr. Ruddy was talking.

"The frost fairy has agreed to extend winter for as long as it is safe for the flora and fauna of the environment," he said. "She cannot come with you into the fairy ring, her priority is to maintain winter. If she does not, spring will come and your kinfolk would then be lost."

I felt my stomach drop into my boots when I heard what he had to say. There was no way in my mind that I could carry out this plan and *not* have it explode in my face… or worse. I almost cried with despair whilst still staring into winter's eyes.

"She has told me, however, that she is willing to give you a gift to abet your efforts."

In one quick movement the frost fairy glided to no more than three inches in front of me. She smelled like pine, and the cold emanating from her body almost froze my nose hairs instantly. She put a hand on my shoulder and spun me around. Her hand was so cold, Bob, I honestly don't know how she didn't want to put on a jacket.

"She is giving you and I the power to fly in her frozen world. No longer will our wings fail us in the frigid winds. But you must keep in mind, Petunia, that like the ice which melts in the sun, her gift will only last for three moons."

With a flutter of her frozen hand, the frost fairy sprinkled something over my wings. It felt cold but warm at the same time, like the loving hand of my mother as she gently tickled my back, making me shiver. I looked back and I wouldn't have believed it if I didn't see it for myself.

My wings sparkled like the frost fairy's. They twinkled and shone in the moonlight, like a thousand tiny diamonds had been fixed to them. I had never seen anything so beautiful in my eleven years of living.

When she was done with me, she did the same thing to Mr. Ruddy. He was even more excited about them than I was, and I watched him almost twirl with delight as he examined his shimmering wings. It took him a second to return to himself. He bowed, with a hint of redness in his cheeks, to the frost fairy in his normal regal manner. She returned his gesture and floated back into the night sky without a single word.

The air seemed somewhat crispier when she left, and the silent darkness of a cold winter's night, returned. The other council members had, at this point, almost turned blue, and Mr. Ruddy ushered them all inside. Even though the temperature didn't seem to affect me anymore, I followed them back into the warmth of the underground.

For a while, Bob, I thought that my lovely new wings would melt in the heat, but they didn't. They carried on sparkling and twinkling in the dim lights of the mushroom tunnels in Sapling Corm. Mr. Ruddy and I suddenly became the subjects of much admiration.

Sparklingly,
Petunia Potterfield.

## Chapter 12 – Two moons past winter's end.

Dear Bob,

I realise now that I am always writing to you to tell you how worried and apprehensive I am. I know I sound like a manic-depressive parrot, and I promise to try and be more positive. I have to really, because I am trying to believe in myself. If the story of Jacinto has taught me anything, it's that even a jinx like me can overcome my curse… at least I hope so for everyone's sake.

With that thought burning in my heart I listened intently when Mr. Ruddy began to teach me the incantation to syphon dream dust. I concentrated whole heartedly on remembering the words. And when he taught me the words to destroy nightmare dust, I concentrated twice as hard. I was determined to recite them word for word with no deviations whatsoever. After my last debacle in Mrs. Scarrowtree's class, I had learned my lesson on overreaching.

According to Mr. Ruddy, these words should never be passed on to anyone other than a new dust collector. Otherwise it might fall into the hands of an unscrupulous fairy who might use them for evil, just like old man Duckweed had. So that's why I've chosen not to write them in your pages, Bob. Anyone could find you and read it.

With that in mind, there was one thing that still bothered me about all of this. I wondered where old man Duckweed heard the incantation from in the first place. I don't think that anyone would have told him by choice. But it was just a fleeing thought, I had more important things to think about.

After what seemed like hours, Mr. Ruddy was finally satisfied with my recital and we embarked on our first journey into the human world. Was I nervous? More than I care to admit even to you, Bob. All I will say is that I had to run to the bathroom three times before we actually left Sapling Corm.

It was snowing outside, but when the flakes landed on my face I didn't feel the usual sting of its coldness. It felt warm and welcoming, for a change, and now I understood why the frost fairy didn't need a jacket.

We fluttered and weaved through the corn fields and over the rooftops of the human's ginormous homes. I collided into a sleeping horse only once along the way. When we finally came to rest, we perched outside of a familiar window. It was Elizabeth's house, and inside she was snuggled up tightly in her warm cosy bed.

I thought that the best human to practice on first would be my friend Elizabeth, although I didn't tell Mr. Ruddy that. I thought he might die from shock if he learned I broke *another* fairy rule. But I knew that if I accidently knocked over a toy, or made too much noise (which was a real possibility), then at least she wouldn't squash me if she woke up.

Mr. Ruddy muttered an incantation to open the widow and I fluttered silently into Elizabeth's warm room. She looked so peaceful while she slept. All around her bed were hand drawn pictures of fairies stuck to her wall, and I recognised one of them as me. I hoped she hadn't told her parents about me, Bob. I'd hate them to think her crazy, because that would be all my fault too.

Mr. Ruddy took a few glances between me and the pictures with narrowed eyes, but he said nothing. Instead, he nodded for me to start. Taking a deep breath, and a fistful of courage, I said the spell quietly at first. I wasn't sure I actually *wanted* it to work. But sure enough, a small tornado of golden sparkles seeped out from Elizabeth's mouth, her eyes, her whole head really, and followed my commands.

Just as quickly as it had come out, it was sucked back into Elizabeth's body again and pulled me with it too. If it wasn't for Mr. Ruddy's steady hand on my shoulder, my whole body would have been sucked toward her face and I would have hit it with a painful smack.

"Dream dust is like a spring, Petunia," he whispered. "You must use your power to cut it from the Bigfoot. Imagine a large knife in your mind, direct your power to the root of the dust and sever the tie. Then it will come loose."

I didn't believe him, but I trusted what he was saying. I repeated the steps, and this time I managed to free the dream dust form Elizabeth's body. I felt kind of mean taking something from her that didn't belong to me, but Mr. Ruddy explained that it was nothing more than the cycle of life. It was no more stealing than eating a berry from a bush to nourish our bodies. I suppose he's right, Bob.

Before we left, however, and while Mr. Ruddy's back was turned, I used one of Elizabeth's colouring sticks to draw a happy face on her picture of me. I had to let her know that I had been to visit.

After that, our search grew more difficult. We peered through many windows to find a child having a nightmare. It was more difficult than I thought it was going to be. Some children laugh and talk in their dreams, but most of them stayed perfectly still regardless of the dream they were having. I knew that if we *did* spot a child having a nightmare, it was probably going to be a doozie.

The stronger the dreams, the more powerful the dream dust. That's one of the reasons dust collectors use children's dreams. A child's imagination is infinitely more powerful and vivid than an adult's. It's also one of the reasons that the nightmare dust is so animated. I have to admit though, Bob, the thought of dealing with nightmare dust had given *me* nightmares, even though I was not asleep.

Just as dawn was approaching, Mr. Ruddy and I found a child who appeared to be in the throes of a terrible dream. He was a young boy about the same age as Elizabeth. He was moaning, groaning, and tossing violently in his bed. With my hands shaking, and Mr. Ruddy a good distance behind me, I entered his room and approached the troubled child.

Suddenly, the boy's hand flew in my direction. I just barely managed to flutter between his fingers and avoid getting smacked against the far wall. Steadying myself again, I took in a deep breath and clenched my fists to stop them shaking before I started. I was so scared that I almost threw up on the unsuspecting child's head then.

Mr. Ruddy gave an impatient cough. Dawn was coming and we were running out of time. The longer I flew there doing nothing, the more likely the child would wake up and see me. So I gathered what little courage I had left and began the chant.

Slowly, I could feel the pull of magic, but it was heavier than Elizabeth's. It was almost like it was trying to drag me down with it and, strangely, I couldn't let it go.

After a few moments a black seething mass floated from the child's body. Once it left him, he curled into a contented slumber while I battled with his nightmare above him. I could feel its strength, Bob. I could feel that it wanted to get me. I breathed hard, my heart pounded, but I didn't give up. As I recited the words to destroy it, it writhed in the air until it finally poofed into a nothingness.

I panted, mostly from disbelief.

"I did it," I shouted.

I probably shouldn't have shouted quiet so loudly because the next thing I knew, the little boy's eyes shot open and he stared at me with wide a frightened expression. He screamed as loudly as he could and hid beneath the covers of his bed. I felt Mr. Ruddy grab my arm and we made a dash for the open window. We got out just before the boy's parents came into the room. It was a close one though. But even *that* couldn't dampen my spirits.

I couldn't help but bask contently in the sunlight as we fluttered back to Sapling Corm. Bob, I was so happy. I *am* so happy. I did it! I actually did it and no one died or exploded. If I can do that, then the story of Jacinto doesn't seem so farfetched to me now. Maybe I *am* like him, more powerful than I thought. Maybe I *can* complete the task that was set in front of me, and I could do it all on my own too.

It won't be long before I find out. My frost wings will only last until tomorrow night and so that's when I'll *have* to do this. I'm too excited to sleep, too apprehensive to eat, but I have to try, because I'll need all of my strength for tomorrow night. Wish me luck, Bob.

Anxiously,
Petunia Pottersfield.

## Chapter 13 – Spring onset.

Dear Bob,

I'm alive! I'm alive and still have all of my fingers and toes too. What a miracle. Let me tell you what happened.

After spending the day napping in Sapling Corm, although my nerves prevented me from sleeping properly, I joined Mr. Ruddy in their Winter's End feast. Even though the fairies of Sapling Corm knew it wasn't quite winter's end, and wouldn't be for a few days yet, they decided to hold the feast regardless. I suppose it might have also been a final farewell to me, just in case I didn't succeed in my mission. It was nice of them, but it only reminded me of what might happen should I fail.

Mr. Ruddy had been so very kind to me whilst I was there, almost like a second father. That night, he made sure that I didn't have much time to think about what I had to do. We spent many wonderful hours dancing together beneath a chandelier of red and green paper ribbons—although, he was by far a better dancer than I.

According to Mr. Ruddy, Sapling Corm would normally be decorated only in green, but the other fairies had intertwined bright red all the way through the underground village, just for me. I could have cried, Bob. I think I did a little. They didn't have to help me or welcome me into their homes, but they did and I loved them all for it.

But the night's festivities eventually had to come to an end, as all good things do. My frosted wings wouldn't wait another night and I was eager to return home, even if to just see what was happening with my family and friend.

I worried about them, Bob. I worried every night since I left them. I wondered if they could think like themselves while they were under Duckweeds nightmare spell. I wondered if they felt abandoned when I left them and they thought me a coward. I had to go back and try and to save them. I had to return to show them that I wasn't a scared little fairy who does nothing but mess-up.

So when the time came, all of the villagers from Sapling Corm walked with me in silence until we came above ground. I could see the worry on their faces, Bob, and it made me doubt myself again. I ran to Mr. Ruddy and hugged him for a long time, not wanting to let go.

"You can do this," he had said to me. "Just remember the story of Jacinto. If he could do it, then I have no doubt in my heart that you can too."

His words cast a bright light on the doubt which hid inside of me like a shadow. I felt braver and more sure then I had in my whole entire life. I asked Mr. Ruddy if I could come back, when this was all over, to let him know what happened. Even though it was forbidden to cross territories, Mr. Ruddy said that I had now been adopted as one of the Sapling Corm fairies, and that I would be welcomed back at any time.

I nearly cried again, Bob. I don't know why I was such a blubbering mess. Maybe it was because he was so nice to me, or the fact that this village had welcomed me with open arms. People didn't run away from me here, they didn't call me "the jinx" they didn't try to stop me when I used magic. No! They wholeheartedly welcomed me and accepted my clumsy ways. Perhaps it was because I hadn't been in their village long enough to cause too much trouble.

I would be lying, Bob, if I didn't say that I had thought about staying in Sapling Corm. I could have stayed in the warmth and protection of their love and forgotten about my own little village. I didn't even have any objections to wearing green. But my heart wouldn't let me. If I stayed I'd be leaving my family, Alisia, and everyone I had ever known to a terrible fate, and this time I *would* only have myself to blame.

So with a thankful and warm heart, and one more hug, I set off on my journey.

I flew into the frosty night determined to not let my fear change my destination or slow me down. I had spent too long in Sapling Corm already and the night was already at its darkest. That was a sure sign the sun was on its way. I had to get there while the village was still sleeping. It was the only way I would be able to syphon the nightmare dust from their bodies.

Along the way I saw the frost fairy. She had been waiting near Furrow Grove to see when I might take on my mammoth task. I suppose she also wanted to know when her season could end. And it *would* end eventually, Bob, whether I succeeded or not.

I passed by her in a flash and I only just barely saw her nod to me. But in my head I heard a whisper which sounded like falling sands made of silver. It twinkled and made me shiver all over as she said "Good luck, young fairy". Her words spurred me on and I found myself flying at speeds I never thought possible, maybe even faster than Blackhawk. And I didn't bump into anything along the way either. Perhaps I really was like Jacinto?

From the air I saw Furrow Grove a little distance off. It looked so different now. The circular mound looked foreboding and the grass and plants around it had all turned black. It looked like someone had put an invisible dome over my village and drained out all of the life from inside. It really looked like the stuff of nightmares, Bob, but I had to face whatever terrors were inside and try to save them all.

I landed at the small opening to the underground tunnels. They were covered with spider webs. Normally spiders steered clear of fairy rings because we have an unwritten understanding with them; they don't try and eat us and we don't turn them into bird food.

However, it looked like the spiders had been drawn to the nightmare world below and had forgotten their fear of us. Their silken webs were strewn throughout the surface of Furrow Grove and it sent a chill up my spine.

I took several deep breaths and pushed past the sticky thread, hoping that the spider which had spun it had long since left. Thankfully, Lady Luck was kind to me for once and no six-legged carnivore came to chase me. I made my way down the narrow corridors of the mushroom tunnels in slow purposeful steps, and searched for any signs of life.

But it was still, Bob. Very still.

I couldn't hear talking, movement, or even the faint sounds of snoring. So I went deeper. Eventually I made my way to Duckweeds chamber and that's where I found them all.

They were huddled together in a mass of sleeping half-fairies. They looked paler than I remembered and thinner too, like they hadn't eaten since I left. I felt a pang of guilt when I saw them. While I had been dancing and enjoying myself, they had been suffering. I don't know how I could have ever contemplated staying in Sapling Corm and leaving them like this.

Fortunately the chamber was tall enough that I didn't have to tip toe between them to get in. As I hovered above their heads I saw my family and Alisia below me. The image of their frail and grey bodies fuelled my determination. I steadied myself for what I had come to do, closed my eyes, and I began my incantation.

Fear gripped my heart with an iron fist. I had only ever done this on a single human child. I don't think anyone in the history of our people has ever syphoned *this* much nightmare dust before. If they had, then they surely never lived to tell about it.

Just as my words finished I felt the unmistakeable tug of the dust. It was stronger than I had ever felt before and I knew I had to disconnect it from the fairies below. But when I opened my eyes, Bob, I nearly lost my wits.

Below me a huge ball of nightmare dust was gathering. It was seeping not only from the fairies, but also from the reserves Duckweed had hidden below the ground. Black lines of snaking sand flowed from between the rocks and gathered with the monster I was creating. It moved and swayed and tried to take form.

I knew I had to be quick. So I used all of my power, and everything else I had inside of me, and cut its ties with its dreamers. I thought I knew fear before this, Bob, but what happened next took years off my life.

The nightmare dust must have smelled my fear, or sensed me above it, because as soon as I set it free it turned its faceless features toward me. Although it didn't have eyes, I could feel it staring at me while it floated in mid-air. I saw arms, legs, a head, and a colossal mouth yawn and grow from its shimmering body. I knew what it was going to do; it was going to try and swallow me whole.

"NOO!" came a roar from the ground. It was old man Duckweed. "No, you can't destroy my plans, I won't let you. I will not fail, not now."

I didn't hang around to find out what he had in store for me. I flew as fast as I could toward the mushroom tunnels and my nightmare monster followed me. It snapped its jaws at my heels and reached a black silty hand in my direction. I darted to the left and just barely escaped its claws. I had nowhere to run or hide. It was dust and could slither between rocks to reach me however small my hiding place might be.

At one point, the beast caught hold of my ankle, pulling me backward. Its claw was icy cold and shocked my skin as though it was made of lightning. I don't know how I did it, but I twisted wildly enough that it lost its grip and I ran again, faster this time.

I was so scared, Bob. My heart beat wildly against my chest and I could barely breathe. I couldn't think for the longest time, and so I just ran. I must have run around the fairy ring three times before my legs started to fail me. I knew I couldn't keep it up.

I had to think of a plan, I had to use my brain and find the answers. From the colossal size of my nightmare monster I knew that the incantation to destroy it wouldn't be enough. It would take an entire fairy ring to destroy *this* monster. If I could only hold it off until morning when the rest of Furrow Grove would wake, then perhaps they could help me. But I suspected that they would probably be too weak to be of any use.

That's when I realised what I had to do.

I darted as fast as my little legs would carry me through the narrow tunnels, dodging and diving around the black sandy arms which appeared from nowhere. I was heading for the surface. I wasn't sure if it would work, but it was the only idea I could think of. So, I trusted myself for the first time ever and followed my instincts.

I burst through the spider webs above the surface and into the night, closely followed by the dark monster. I hovered above the lifeless village of Furrow Grove and began the incantation to destroy it. I knew the monster was too powerful to destroy by myself, but I was hoping that I would be able to just hold it there: Hold it long enough for my plan to work.

I repeated the incantation over, and over again and the nightmare monster squirmed under my spell. It didn't die, but it didn't move either. My arms weakened, the cold of the early morning seeped into my wings again, and I cried out against the strain of it all. But never once did I stop my incantations and the slithering, reaching mass of darkness remained trapped.

Out of the corner of my eye I saw the fairies of Furrow Grove begin to emerge from the underground tunnels. I was right, they were weak and couldn't fly. Some of them leaned on the others as they looked toward me. When they saw what I was doing, something magical happened and my breath hitched in my chest when I saw.

Each one of the dust collectors, including my mother, raised their hands in the air toward the monster and repeated my incantation. The other fairies around them heard the words and followed their lead. The all believed in me, Bob. They saw what I was doing and they followed my lead.

My bottom lip quivered and my eyes blurred with tears as we joined forces. A chorus of magical words shot through the air and into the nightmare dust, making it writhe in pain even more. But still it didn't die, we weren't strong enough. I felt the familiar hot pain flow from the dust and into my body as it struggled to live, but I didn't waiver. I gritted my teeth and chanted even louder.

That's when I saw it, and I had never been happier to see it in my whole life. It was the sun. Glints of gold and orange light streamed from the horizon and lit Furrow Grove in a dazzling display of brightness. The nightmare monster turned to me. I could feel the bubbling hatred emanating as though it knew what was going to happen.

I remembered, from my own nightmares, that bad dreams seem to disappear when the sun came up, and I was hoping that it would be the same for my nightmare monster.

It tried to squirm away from the daylight, but we held it firmly in place. The sun beams shone brightly through its black dust and through its body like spears. It let out a harrowing howl before it suddenly exploded into a thousand shadowy diamonds. The diamonds turned to nothing as they floated to the ground below in the deafening silence of morning.

I did it, Bob. *We* did it. The nightmare dust monster was no more and I couldn't help but give a triumphant yell and pump my fists in the air. Exhausted and weary, I flew down to my family, and to Alisia, who greeted me with open arms.

I burst into deep, shuddering sobs then, Bob. I couldn't help it. All of the fear, the doubt and the worry that had followed me all of my life… was gone. That's when my parents cried with utter joy and pride for me for the first time in my life, and I will remember those tears forever.

Even though they were weak with hunger and weary from their own ordeal, the townsfolk of Furrow Grove lifted me into the air and cheered. In that moment Bob, I was their hero.

Jubilantly,
Petunia Pottersfield.

## Chapter 14 – Three moons later

Dear Bob,

It's a horrible fate, but what choice did they have? "What are you talking about?" I hear you ask.

Well, after the nightmare monster was defeated, the F.P.A. caught old man Duckweed. I think he knew he was going to be in big trouble and was trying to escape through an underground tunnel he had dug. It led out into the forest and if he had gotten that far, we would have never found him again.

He was dragged, kicking and shouting vile insults all the way to the council chambers, where Alisia's dad and four others sat at the high table. It was remarkable how similar the rooms and proceedings were to Sapling Corm's... with the exception of the red robes instead of green.

I was allowed to sit at the back of the room on one of the benches while the trial took place. I kind of felt like I had to really, people were expecting the "hero of Furrow Grove" to be there. I had turned into a bit of a celebrity in my village, which was strange in itself. I couldn't walk to school without at least ten hands clapping me on the back and congratulating me on a "fine job".

It also meant that sneaking out to visit Elizabeth was difficult too, but I managed it on one occasion. We played tea parties and I made her toys fly in the air. I think I've really come to like that human. At least she didn't follow me around town trying to shake my hand, like the other fairies. I'm not sure I liked all the attention, but Alisia insisted that I couldn't *not* turn up to the trial and see the end to it all. Some fairies were, apparently, going just so they could get to see me. What a turn-up for the books.

Mr. Blossom rapped the gavel on his table to demand order from the noisy chamber. He had the same red hair and wild lilac eyes as Alisia, only his were far more stern.

There was a mix of angry and excited fairies in the chambers that day, although I think most of them were just angry.

"Bernard Duckweed," he began. "You have been brought before the high council, charged with endangering the lives of fairies, conspiring to commit atrocities against the natural order, and hoarding prohibited magic dust. We all have born witness to your crimes and therefore you have been found guilty. However, in the interests of fairness you will be allowed to speak on your own behalf so that you might defend your actions."

Silence followed Mr. Blossom's statement and old man Duckweed eyed his spectators with his dark black eyes. He stopped when he met mine and began to speak.

"I was once like you, all of you. I had a lovely home, a job as a dust collector, a wife, and I was happy." That's how he must have learned how to syphon dream dust, Bob. I was glad that, at least, that there wasn't another cohort in his plan.

"Most of you probably don't remember the Bigfoot invasion, do you?" he continued. "No, of course you don't. You're all too young to remember. But I do because I was there. One hundred and twenty three years ago our village was trodden and stomped on by some reckless Bigfoot who paid no more heed to our lives then a bird would to the air beneath its wings."

I had no idea old man Duckweed was quite so *old.* He must have been the oldest fairy in Furrow Grove. "My lovely wife, my Ivy, was killed in that attack, and do know how they got justice for her? They did nothing. NOTHING!"

Old man Duckweed paced the floor but kept his eyes firmly fixed on me.

"How was I meant to continue life without my Ivy? But I was. I was expected to carry on living, giving to nature and hiding from the very monsters that had killed her. Well I decided that I wouldn't. I learned everything I could possible learn about the dark magic from the stories of old, and it elongated my life. I gathered as much nightmare dust as I dared, and I waited.

"I bided my time until I was ready, and then I made all of you my slaves. If you didn't have the stomach to help me get revenge on these Bigfoots back then, then I was going to *make* you do it now."

It was at that point that he pointed his bony finger at me and sneered with a deadly and dangerous smile.

"And if it wasn't for this catastrophic mess of a fairy, my plan would have worked. You have made yourself a powerful enemy, young girl. Mark my words, we shall meet again and this time you won't fair out so well."

His words sent a shiver down my spine, Bob. I knew then, and I know still, that he meant every word he said. From the evidence of his actions so far, I knew he was capable of carrying out his threat too. That's probably why Mr. Blossom handed down the most severe punishment he could. Old man Duckweed was to have his wings clipped and would be banished from Furrow Grove, forever.

But along with being utterly terrified of him, I also felt a little sorry for him. Was that wrong of me? I suppose no one really knows what someone else is feeling, or why they do horrible things to one another. But when I imagined old man Duckweed smiling with a loving wife I also imagined the pain he must have felt when he lost her. It would be enough to wither the heart of the most gallant fairy.

Old man Duckweed was taken away then, but his words lingered with me and probably will for the rest of my life. The only comfort I could take is that he is very, very old, and I might outlive him and his vengeance. It was little comfort, but I took it nonetheless.

It was when I was leaving the council chambers that something very peculiar happened. It wasn't a terribly bad thing, but it was embarrassing. In my contemplations I didn't look where I was going and I tripped over someone's foot. When I fell to the floor I must have accidently let out some magic, or sneezed, or something, because when I looked up, everyone in the chamber had a curly piggy tail coming from their bottoms... including me.

My heart sank, Bob.

I thought my fight with Lady Luck was over. But it seems that that was not to be the case. I didn't understand what was going on. Had my good fortune just been a coincidence? I had to find out if the same thing had happened to Jacinto, so the next morning I flew to Sapling Corm—without the knowledge of the council or my family.

That's when I met my wonderful Mr. Ruddy again and told him everything that had happened with the nightmare dust. The people of Sapling Corm cheered and celebrated, and I could see there was a genuine look of relief in everyone's eyes. They laid out a sumptuous picnic for me and we danced for hours.

Once the celebrations died down I found a quiet corner to talk to Mr. Ruddy. I told him that despite my victory I seemed to be as clumsy as ever and asked him if the same was true of Jacinto. You'll never guess what he told me, Bob.

"There is no Jacinto," he said. "It was just a story I made up at that very moment. Sometimes, Petunia, when our minds are muddled up in self-doubt, panic, or worry, it can blind us to the things that are obvious to others. I knew I didn't have time to help you see this, so I invented someone that *you* could believe in... instead of yourself. Now you see that you could have done it by yourself all along."

Was he right? Was my magic all muddled up from self-doubt? Perhaps now that I know this I will believe in myself a little more. I also know, however, that accidents happen and more often than not, they happen to me. Maybe I will always be a little clumsy and occasionally my potions will still explode, but now that I have seen what I can do with some self-confidence, I know that I can also do great things too.

Confidently,
Petunia Pottersfield.

To be released in 2017


Dear Bob,

Petunia Pottersfield and the Changing Stone